The Story Book

Character Building Stories for Children

Arthur S. Maxwell

REVIEW AND HERALD® PUBLISHING ASSOCIATION

Since 1861 | www.reviewandherald.com

Cover illustration by John Steel

R&H Cataloging Service
Maxwell, Arthur Stanley, 1896-1970.
    The story book: character building
stories for children.

    1. Values—Juvenile works.   I. Title.

                /70

ISBN 978-0-8280-0539-5

CONTENTS

LESSON INDEX

Mother's Hands

JUST WHEN IT HAPPENED I do not know. Maybe fifty years ago, maybe a hundred. It really doesn't matter. The story was old when I was a boy and that's quite some time ago now. I tell it again because you will love it, too.

A sweet young mother, having laid her baby girl to sleep in her cradle, went down the street to visit a neighbor. She had often left her baby before, just for a few minutes, and there had been no trouble; so she had no doubt that all would be well now.

Arriving at the neighbor's house, she began to chat about this and that, but was suddenly interrupted by a sound that always sent a chill through her, the city fire alarm.

"Don't worry," said the neighbor. "Most likely it's only a grass fire. There are lots of them at this time of year."

But the alarm sounded again and again.

"It must be serious," said the mother.

"Oh, don't bother," said the neighbor. "I'm sure the fire isn't anywhere near here."

"But listen!" said the mother. "I can hear the fire engine, and it is coming this way. And look! See the people running.

They are running down this street. They are running toward my house!"

Without another word she dashed into the street and ran with the gathering crowd.

Then she saw it. Her own house was on fire! Smoke and flames were already pouring through the roof.

"My baby!" she cried frantically. "My baby!"

The crowd was thick around the house, but like one gone mad she pushed and tore her way through.

"My baby! My baby! My little Margie!"

A fireman seized her.

"You can't go!" he cried. "You will be burned to death."

"Let me go! Let me go!" she cried, breaking free and dashing into the flaming house.

She knew just where to go. Running through the smoke and flames, she seized her precious baby, then turned to make her way out. But, overcome by the smoke, she swayed and fell, and would have burned to death with her baby had not a fireman seized her and carried her out.

What a cheer went up as they appeared! But alas, though the baby was saved unharmed, the poor mother was badly hurt. Kind friends put her in an ambulance and hurried her off to the hospital. There it was found that her hands, the brave, dear hands that had lifted her baby from the blazing crib, were terribly burned. All their beauty, of which she had

been so proud, was gone. Though the doctors did their best to save them, they were left marred and crippled.

Months later the brave mother was released from the hospital. She and her baby were together again in a new home.

Weeks became months, and months became years. The baby toddled, walked, ran. She was no longer a baby; she was a little girl. She was beginning to notice things.

One day when Marjorie was eight years old, her mother was washing dishes in the kitchen sink.

Suddenly Marjorie saw something that she had always seen but never noticed before.

"Mother," she exclaimed, "what ugly hands you have!"

"Yes, dear," said Mother quietly, though hurt almost beyond words. "They are ugly, aren't they?"

"But why do you have ugly hands when other people have pretty hands?" said Marjorie, not knowing how every word was like a dagger in Mother's heart.

Tears filled Mother's eyes.

"Oh!—what have I done wrong?" asked Marjorie.

Then Mother took Marjorie's hand and led her to the davenport. "There's something I must tell you, dear," she said.

Then she told her story, as Marjorie had never understood it before. She told of the fire, of the people who tried to hold her back, of the wild dash into the burning house, how she lifted the baby from the flaming crib, how she fell,

how she was rescued, and how badly she had been burned.

"My hands were beautiful till then," she said.

Marjorie clasped the crooked hands in hers, tears streaming down her cheeks. "Mother dear," she cried, "they are the most beautiful hands in all the world!"

Children, there are other hands that were wounded for you. The hands of Jesus, the children's Friend and Saviour; the hands of Him who came down from heaven to rescue His people from sin and save them in His beautiful kingdom.

You know what happened to Jesus. Evil men drove great nails through His hands and hung Him on a cross to die.

Then they buried Him in Joseph's new tomb. But they couldn't keep Him there. He rose again and ascended to heaven, where He lives today, waiting for the glad day when He shall return.

The marks of the nails are still there. When He comes back they will still be there. We shall know Him then "by the print of the nails in His hands."

Those nailmarks will be there through all eternity. As you meet Him in the New Jerusalem or in the lovely new earth, you will know that those hands, those dear, dear hands of Jesus, were marred that you might be 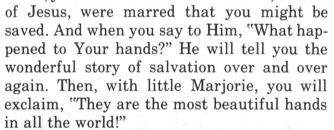 saved. And when you say to Him, "What happened to Your hands?" He will tell you the wonderful story of salvation over and over again. Then, with little Marjorie, you will exclaim, "They are the most beautiful hands in all the world!"

When Dick Ran Away

DICK WAS UPSET AGAIN. In fact, it seemed that he was always getting upset about something. If he did not get his own way all the time, he would carry on in the most hateful manner. And if anyone corrected him, he would either snarl an angry reply, or else wander off into some corner and sulk.

When in these very bad moods he would mutter threats about running away from home. Although he was only 10 years old, he had a very big opinion of himself and was quite sure that he was well able to look after himself anywhere. That he owed his father and mother anything for all their loving care for him never seemed to enter his mind. He only wanted to get away from all control, away to some place where he would be able to do just as he pleased.

He was thinking these thoughts now. Daddy had asked him to mow the lawn just as he had planned to go out and play ball with the boy next door. How he hated mowing the lawn! Why should he mow the lawn? He wished there were no lawn to cut. He would give anything to get away from the sight of it. But he did mow it, seething with rebellion.

That afternoon his wishes were crossed again. Several times, in fact. As a result he became rude and cross, and finished up with a good spanking and being sent early to bed. He did not say his prayers, and instead of going to sleep, he planned what seemed an exciting dash for liberty. He would get up when everyone else had gone to bed, creep out of the house, and run far, far away. He was not quite sure where he would go, or what he would do when he got there. He had only one desire—to get away where there would be no lawn to mow and where he wouldn't have to give up things for his brothers and sisters, nor be expected to do what he was told.

At last, when all was still, and he felt sure that everyone must be fast asleep, he decided to put his plan into action.

So he crawled softly out of bed, put on his clothes very quietly, took his billfold out of the drawer—he was very proud of this billfold, for it contained a whole dollar—and crept silently out of his room.

As he passed the bed where his baby brother was lying asleep, it occurred to him that he would never see little Tiny again, so he bent over and kissed him. A strange lump came into his throat, and he couldn't swallow very well. He kissed Tiny twice, and then went out of the room. Going past the room where Daddy and Mother were asleep, he thought he would like to say good-by to Mother anyway. He wasn't quite sure about Daddy, because he had made him mow the lawn. But he wouldn't like it if he couldn't see Mother again.

He began to wonder whether he should run away after all. Then the old, hard spirit came back, and he went downstairs. Very quietly he unlocked the front door, and went out into the cool night air.

He stopped on the doorstep. This was hardly what he had dreamed about. It was too dark for one thing, and too chilly for another. Bed began to seem very nice. Perhaps, after all, it would be better to go back.

But no, he wouldn't. He closed the door. There was a snap! and he realized that he couldn't go back now even if he wanted to. That wasn't a nice feeling at all. He wished he hadn't let the door close quite so tightly.

It was done now, however, and he must go. He went down
to the front gate and out into the street. There was nobody
about. All was very quiet and still. The sky was black, and
the only light came from the street lights. It was all rather
frightening. Dick didn't like it a bit. If the door weren't
locked, he told himself, he would go back to bed.

He walked some distance down the street, and as the cold
night air cooled his fevered mind, he began to realize more
and more what a foolish enterprise he had started on. "If the
boys at school get to hear about this," he said to himself,
"they'll tease me for the rest of the year." The very thought of
such a thing made him turn around suddenly and make for
home as fast as he could.

He had not gone far, however, when he nearly jumped out
of his skin as a heavy hand was laid on his shoulder and a
strange voice spoke to him.

"What are you doing out at this time of night?" asked the
policeman.

Dick was paralyzed with fright. He had not expected this. Words would not come. He merely struggled to get free.

"You'd better come along with me," said the policeman. "You've been up to some mischief, it seems."

"I haven't, I haven't," gasped Dick. "I've made a mistake, that's all, please, sir."

"I should think you have made a mistake, being out here at one o'clock in the morning. You can tell me all about it when we get down to the station."

"You're not going to take me to the police station, are you?" cried Dick, more frightened still. "Let me go home! I want to go home."

"You'll go home, all right," said the policeman, "after we have had a little chat."

And so poor Dick found himself for the first time in his life on his way to the police station!

There he was asked more questions in ten minutes than any teacher had ever asked him at school. He was frightened, wondering what the policeman was going to do with him and what his daddy would say.

How he wished he had never started out on such a foolish venture! Finally, the policeman took him home. How very small poor Dick felt! What a homecoming! What would the others say?

Daddy, in his pajamas, opened the door. It startled him to see Dick there, and with a policeman!

"What in the world!" he began.

The policeman explained and departed, smiling. Dick jumped into Daddy's arms and hugged him, pajamas and all. They didn't say much to each other, but just walked up the stairs like that to tell Mother all about it.

When Dick got up for breakfast that morning he found his favorite food—crispy waffles, with delicious applesauce —waiting for him. Mother had it ready because, she said, her little prodigal had returned, so she surely had to kill the fatted calf. (See the story in Volume 1 called "The Boy Who Ran Away From Home.")

And as for Dick, he said very earnestly that he had run away for the last time in his life, and that he certainly wouldn't even think about doing so again.

Vera's Victory

VERA WAS ONE of those very lively little girls—you know the kind. Full of high spirits. Always getting into mischief. The kind that makes Mother tired and gives Father headaches.

This particular afternoon Vera had been a little more lively than usual, and when the time came for her to go to bed no one was more happy than her mother.

"At last!" sighed Mother, as she went downstairs after tucking Vera into bed and kissing her good night. "Now, perhaps, I can have a little peace."

Mother went into the dining room, now quiet and still. Feeling very tired, she decided to lie on the sofa for a little while and take a rest. Gradually she felt herself falling asleep. Then, before her eyes were quite closed, something began to happen.

Very slowly, very softly, the dining room door began to open. A little more, and a little more.

Who could it be? thought Mother, frightened. Had a burglar gotten into the house?

Then, what do you suppose? From behind the door came a

white-robed figure. Yes, it was little Vera in her nightie.

Mother did not move. Nor did she say a word. She just pretended to be asleep, and watched.

Vera tiptoed across the soft carpet over to the dining table.

Now, in the middle of the table was a large bowl of apples, oranges, and nuts. On top of all was a big bunch of grapes. Vera had been looking at this bunch of grapes all day, wishing that it might be hers. Now she reached out her hand, picked up the grapes, and tiptoed out of the room, closing the door very quietly behind her.

Of course she thought that nobody had seen her. But Mother, as usual, had seen everything. Mother always does!

But now Mother felt very sad.

"To think that my Vera would do a thing like that!" she said to herself. "To think that my own little girl would wait till she thought I was not looking and then creep down here

to steal that bunch of grapes! Oh dear, what shall I do? What shall I say to her?"

Then, just as Mother was feeling very much upset, something began to happen again.

Once more the dining room door began to open—very softly, very slowly. From behind it came the same little white-robed figure. It was Vera again, still in her nightie, and still clasping the bunch of grapes tightly in her hand.

Tiptoeing over to the table, she put the bunch of grapes back in exactly the same place that she had found it. Then, in a big, loud voice, she said, "And there, Mr. Devil, that's where you get left."

After that she turned around and started for the door. But before she had reached it, Mother was on her feet and her arms were clasped around Vera's neck.

"Oh, darling!" she cried. "I'm so glad you won the victory over that temptation!"

What a happy time they both had then!

I like to think of what must have happened on the stairs that evening. All the way up, the voice of the tempter had said, "Go on, Vera; grapes have a lovely taste. Take one. Nobody will know. It will be all right. Mother will never find out."

At the same time another voice inside her had said, "No, don't, Vera. That would be stealing. That would be wrong. Mother wouldn't like it. Be a good girl and take those grapes back! Put them back where you found them."

Somewhere on the stairs the victory was won. And after that everything turned out happily—as it always does when we fight temptation and win.

Every boy and girl is tempted at some time or other to do something wrong. Sometimes the temptation is very strong indeed. Sometimes you may wonder what *is* the right thing to do. But if you listen to that little voice that speaks within your heart, the voice of conscience, you will not make a mistake. Jesus will give you the victory, if you ask His help.

The Hollow Pie

ROBERT HAD THE VERY bad habit of always taking the biggest and best of everything for himself. His brothers, Charlie and Ted, would call him all sorts of names for doing it, but that did not seem to make any difference.

Mother was very sorry about it, too, especially since Robert, when invited out to parties, always disgraced the family by his greediness. What could be done? Mother talked the matter over with her sister, who lived on the next street.

A few days later the boys were delighted to receive an invitation to dinner from their aunt. Remembering all the good things they had enjoyed there in times past, they looked forward to the day of the party.

At last the day came and dinnertime arrived—for which Robert especially had been waiting.

The table was piled with good things. What Robert looked at longingly were the cupcakes, jellies, small pies, and chocolates.

Robert's eyes gazed excitedly on the wonderful spread of

tasty dishes. Oh, my! he thought, if only I could attend to this little matter all by myself!

He looked at everything and made up his mind which of them he would choose when they were passed around.

When all the visitors had been given their places at the table, dinner began. They all began with bread and potatoes and greens in the usual way, but Robert soon got tired of that. He looked at the plate of small pies, one whole pie for each person. He wanted that biggest one. Would he get it in time, or would Charlie get it first?

The pies were passed around. Charlie and Ted took small ones and opened them. What wonderful centers they have! thought Robert. Now, if only I can get that big one.

Robert's turn came. The biggest pie was still there, and of course he took it with joy.

But a disappointment awaited him. As he cut through the top, the whole pie collapsed. It was hollow!

Poor Robert! Tears filled his eyes, but no one seemed to notice what had happened. He ate the crust as bravely as he could and said nothing.

The cupcakes were passed round. Robert thought he was

quite justified in taking the biggest this time, seeing that there had been nothing in his pie.

But something was wrong with his cake. It looked all right outside, but the center was bitter. What can be the matter? thought Robert. Auntie was generally a good cook. And then, too, the others didn't seem to be having any trouble at all. It wasn't fair, thought Robert, but he didn't dare say anything for fear the others would laugh at him.

Nobody seemed to notice Robert's unhappiness, and no one passed him anything to make up for his bad luck. In fact, the others all seemed to be enjoying themselves to the full.

The chocolates came next, and by this time Robert was getting desperate. "I'll have to make up for lost time by taking those two big beauties in the center," he said to himself as he removed the two largest, best-looking ones from the plate.

"Ugh!" said Robert, groaning inwardly and blushing all over with disappointment. "What a horrible taste!"

Swallowing one with difficulty, he tried the other to take the taste away, only to find it worse.

On the way home Charlie remarked to Robert about the splendid dinner they had had.

"Splendid *what?*" said Robert.

"I thought you weren't enjoying yourself," said Charlie; "you looked uncomfortable. What was the matter?"

"Matter?" said Robert. "Everything I took was bad, even when I took what looked best every time."

"Maybe that was the cause of the trouble, Robert," said Charlie knowingly. "I think if I were you I'd leave the biggest and best-looking things for somebody else next time."

That night Robert stayed awake quite a long time. There were two reasons. One was a pain under his pajama jacket, and the other the advice Charlie had given him. He put two and two together and at last decided that the best and safest course for him would be to follow Charlie's suggestion in the future.

Peter Pays Up

PETER WAS STAYING with his grandma, and early one afternoon she suggested that they go shopping together. Peter was delighted. Very soon the two were on their way.

On arriving at the neighborhood grocery store, they went inside and were met with a cheery "Good afternoon" from Mrs. Green, the smiling saleswoman behind the counter. Grandma went over to talk to her and buy the things she had written down on her list while Peter wandered around looking at all the goods for sale.

What a lot of beautiful things there were! In one corner, under a glass case, there was a pile of fresh brown loaves of bread, and the most tempting cakes and pies. In a refrigerator there were cartons of milk and packages of butter and cheese. Piled up on shelves there were all sorts of bright-colored cartons. In the center of the floor were baskets of fruit and vegetables. Altogether they made a very pleasant picture, and the mixture of delicious aromas made Peter very, very hungry.

Maybe you know how it feels to be five years old, to take

◄ Painting by William Dolwick

Five-year-old Peter's love for blackberries got him into trouble, and taught him a lesson he never forgot.

a long walk, and then go into a store full of food. Well, Peter felt just like that.

It so happened that among the baskets of fruit there were several filled with big luscious blackberries. How Peter did love blackberries! He never could get enough of them, and now here in front of him were more than he had ever seen before.

He put out his hand to take one, but a little voice inside him seemed to say, "No, Peter; you mustn't do that; that would be stealing." But the berries looked so delicious that he felt he *had* to take one. After all, he thought, there were so many, many berries that nobody would ever notice if he was to take just one.

So Peter did not listen to his conscience. Instead, he put out one hand and took just one blackberry. But that one tasted so good that he decided to take another one. How sweet it was!

Then, seeing that there seemed to be just as many left in the basket as there had been before, he took one from another basket. And another. In fact, he was just getting settled to a real meal of blackberries when he heard a familiar voice from the other side of the store.

"Peter! Peter! Where are you?" called Grandma.

"Here I am, Grandma," cried Peter, wiping his hands on the back of his trousers and hurrying around the pile of baskets.

"Come along, dear," said Grandma. "We're all ready to go home now. Would you like to carry one of the bags? How good you have been all the time while Grandma has been shopping!"

Peter blushed a little at this as he took the bag Grandma handed to him. Then they opened the door and went out.

As they walked along Grandma suddenly stopped.

"Peter," she said, "look at me!"

Peter looked up, trying to appear as innocent as possible.

"What are those black marks on your face, Peter?" asked Grandma.

"What black marks?" asked Peter.

"All around your mouth. Not quite black, but blackish red."

"I don't know," said Peter, although if he could have seen his dirty face, he would have owned up right away.

"Peter, you have been eating blackberries," said Grandma. "Haven't you?"

Peter's head went down. "Just one or two," he said.

"Where did you get them?" asked Grandma.

"In the store," said Peter.

"Did Mrs. Green say you could have them?"

"No."

"Do you mean you took them without asking?"

"Yes."

"Then Peter was a very naughty boy," said Grandma, "and I am very much ashamed of him. Come along, let's go home, and we will see what should be done about it."

Peter began to cry, and it was a very sad walk they had together, so different from the journey they had taken but a little while before.

When they got indoors Grandma took Peter on her knee and told him how very wrong it is to take things that belong to other people; that it is breaking the commandment which says, "Thou shalt not steal." She also told him that there

were just two things he had to do. One was to ask God to forgive him and the other was to go to Mrs. Green, pay her for the berries he had eaten, and tell her how sorry he was that he had taken them.

"I don't mind asking God to forgive me," said Peter, crying; "but I don't want to ask Mrs. Green."

"I know it's hard," said Grandma; "but it's the only way. Now go and find your purse."

"You mean I have to pay for the berries myself?"

"Surely you must," said Grandma.

"But it will take all my money," said Peter.

"Never mind if it takes all you have," said Grandma. "You must make it right. But I don't think it will take all. In fact, I think a dime would pay for all you ate."

"A whole dime!" said Peter. "Do I have to give Mrs. Green a whole dime?"

"Yes," said Grandma. "And the sooner you go down to see her the better. Wipe your eyes now and be a big, brave boy."

Peter wiped them with the backs of his hands, and Grandma kissed him good-by. Holding his dime tightly he set off for the grocery store.

How far away it seemed as he dragged one weary foot after the other! But at last the store came in sight and, with his heart beating hard, he went inside.

"What! Back again so soon!" exclaimed Mrs. Green. "Did Grandma forget something?"

"No," said Peter slowly, "I did."

"You did!" said Mrs. Green. "What did you forget?"

"Mrs. Green, er—er—I—er—er—please, I forgot to pay for the blackberries I ate. And—er—er—please, Grandma said they're worth a dime. So I've brought it out of my very own money and—er—er—please, I'm very sorry I didn't ask you about them first."

And with that Peter put the dime on the counter, turned

around, and ran for the door. Opening it, he dashed outside and started to run home. But he had not gone far when he heard Mrs. Green calling him.

"Peter!" she said. "I want you a minute. Come back here."

Very slowly Peter went back, as if expecting to be scolded.

"You forgot something else," said Mrs. Green, smiling, and handing him a paper bag.

"No," said Peter, "I didn't leave that."

"But it's for you, anyway," said Mrs. Green. "Just something good for your supper." Then she patted him on the head and told him to run home quickly. Peter thought he saw tears in her eyes, but he wasn't quite sure, and he couldn't think why.

How he did run then! It seemed as though he was home almost before he had started.

"Look what she gave me!" he cried. "Grandma, look!"

Grandma looked. It was a big delicious-looking doughnut with jam inside.

"Aren't you glad you went back and made things right?" said Grandma.

"Am I!" exclaimed Peter.

"It's always the best thing to do," said Grandma.

The Two Carolines

CAROLINE HERMAN WAS a very nice little girl in many ways. She had pretty hair and big blue eyes, and when she was all dressed and ready to start out for school you would have thought, to look at her, that there wasn't a nicer little girl in all the world.

But there were two Carolines. One was the home Caroline and the other was the school Caroline. The home Caroline was left on the doorstep every morning and picked up every dinnertime when the school Caroline came back.

Now, the home Caroline was a cross, pouty, grumbly, growly, and disobedient Caroline, quite unlike the Caroline that everybody saw outside and thought was such a nice little girl.

Mother was worried almost to tears over her two Carolines. What could she do?

Now, Caroline loved her schoolteacher very much. Indeed, by the way she acted, it seemed as if she loved her teacher more than she did even her own mother. She would take flowers and other pretty things to her to show her affection, and of course the teacher, seeing only the school

Painting by Vernon Nye, © Review and Herald ▶

Outside of her home, everybody thought Caroline was a sweet, courteous girl. At home she was quite a different person.

VERNON
NYE '48

Caroline, thought she must always be a very good girl.

One day the school Caroline came home and changed suddenly on the doorstep, as usual, into the home Caroline. After a while Mother called to her, "Will you please go around to the store and buy me some groceries? Here is the list."

"No, don't want to, I'm tired," snapped the home Caroline.

However, she finally decided to go under protest.

While she was gone, a visitor came to see Mrs. Herman to plan for the next parent-teachers' meeting, and was invited to stay for dinner.

"Just make yourself at home in the living room," said Mrs. Herman, "while I do a little in the kitchen. You can write at my desk and I'll leave the door open so we can talk."

In a few minutes Caroline came into the kitchen, slamming the back door as she entered and grumbling about the heavy groceries.

"Here are your old things," she said, throwing them down on the floor. "Now I'm going out to play."

"But Mother's tired; wouldn't you like to help her finish her work?"

"No, I don't want to."

"Well, please set the table for dinner."

"Don't want to."

"But you must do something to help Mother. Please set the table, Caroline."

"Oh, I hate setting the table," said Caroline, slamming the door and putting on a pout that would almost frighten anyone. Pulling out the tablecloth from the drawer with many grumblings, she spread it out in a rough-and-tumble sort of way. Then she brought out the knives and forks, scattered them among a few dishes, and prepared to walk off.

Mother looked displeased, but did not say anything until Caroline was about to go. Then she said, "Caroline, set an

extra place at the table. We are having a visitor to dinner tonight. In fact, you might speak to her now. She's in the living room."

Startled, Caroline looked around and noticed that the living room door was open.

"But, Mother dear"—her tone had suddenly changed—"the table is not set for visitors."

"No, but it is set for Mother."

"But, Mother, I would like to arrange it better."

"It is too late now. We must not keep our visitor waiting. Please call her in."

Trembling a little, Caroline went into the living room.

"Mother says, Will you please———"

She stopped. It was her teacher!

"Oh, Teacher, have you heard all I have been saying? Oh, dear!" cried Caroline, bursting into tears.

"I am sorry my little Caroline is not the same at home as she is at school," said Teacher.

"Oh, I'm so sorry!" wept Caroline. "I won't ever be so naughty again."

And, really, to tell the truth she never was.

A Boy in Chains

THE OTHER DAY I saw a strange sight in New York City. Yes, it was a boy in chains.

"What!" you say, "a boy in chains nowadays?"

Yes, a real, live slave boy, despite the fact that Abraham Lincoln freed the slaves a long time ago.

The boy was quite small, which made me think that he was very young, but his face had a strange, oldish look, so that I couldn't tell just what his age might be. As I looked at him, I was struck with the fact that he was puffing away at a cigarette like a grownup. So I decided to speak to him.

"How is it that you are smoking at your age?" I asked him kindly.

"Can't help it, mister," he replied, with amazing frankness.

"Can't help it?" I repeated. "That's very strange. How old are you?"

"Just thirteen."

"Just thirteen!" I exclaimed. "Then how long have you been smoking?"

"Three years."

"Three years!" I said, astonished. "You mean to tell me you have been smoking since you were ten?"

"Yes. The other boys smoked, so I started too."

"What other boys?"

"All the boys in my grade at school. And most of the seventh-graders smoke too."

"And the sixth?"

"Yes, mister, some in the sixth. I know; I've seen them."

I was amazed, wondering how many boy slaves to the smoking habit there must be in the country nowadays.

"And now I suppose you can't give it up," I said.

"Right. I can't. I've tried, but it's no use."

"Then you're a slave," I said.

"That's about it. I am."

A slave at thirteen!

"You'll be terribly sorry later on," I said. "You are poisoning yourself. You will never be able to do well in play or in work if you go on like this."

"I know," he said. "Sort of gets your wind; you can't run so fast. I've felt it myself out on the school playground."

So he had noticed the terrible effect of tobacco already. At thirteen!

Poor little slave!

We talked on awhile about the harm that smoking does, and the importance of breaking the habit right away.

"You will have to call up all your will power," I said to him, "and put your foot down now."

"Maybe after I have smoked these," he said, pointing to the big pack that was bulging from his pocket.

"No," I said firmly. "If you want to stop it there's only one time to do it."

"And that's now," he said with a smile. "I know."

That raised my hopes.

"You're right, son," I said. "You have the idea. Stop now, and throw the rest away. Will you?"

"I think I will," he said.

"Good boy!" I replied. "Promise me that you'll never touch the horrid things again."

"All right."

We shook hands on it, and I sent up a little prayer that Jesus would help him in the struggle he was bound to have.

As we parted there was a brave look on his face.

My little slave friend had come very near to freedom. His chains were unloosed.

Did he step out of them into a new life of liberty?

Did he keep his promise?

I rather think he did.

Digging for a Bicycle

WHOEVER HEARD OF such a thing! Digging for a bicycle, indeed! What next?

But it's true. He did dig for it.

"Then it must have been all rusty when he found it," you say.

Oh, no, it wasn't. It was just as bright and shiny as it could possibly be, all brand new and beautiful.

It happened this way.

Bobby, who was just 11 years old, had been wanting a bicycle for a very long time. In fact, he had asked his daddy for one over and over again. But every time he had asked, Daddy had said, "Sorry, Bobby, but there's no money to buy bicycles just now. I'm afraid you'll have to wait a bit longer."

So Bobby had waited and waited, and meanwhile all his friends got bicycles, some as Christmas presents and some as birthday presents. "Isn't there some way I could earn enough money to buy one?" he said.

"Now you're talking some good, sound sense," said Daddy. "That's the best way I know to get money for the things we think we need. Earn it! And if you do earn that bicycle,

Bobby, let me tell you that you will enjoy it ten times more than if it were given you by a rich uncle."

"But what can I do to earn the money?" asked Bobby.

"Well," said Daddy, "I am very anxious to have the garden dug, and because I do not have time to dig it myself, I'll have to get someone to dig it for me. Now, if you would dig it as deeply and thoroughly as anyone else, taking out the worst of the weeds, then I would be glad to contract with you for the job."

"And will you really pay me the same as you would pay anyone else?" asked Bobby, a little doubtfully.

"I will," said Daddy. "You'll take longer than a man with a rotary tiller, but the total amount I will pay for the job will be just the same as I would give him. Now, Bobby, what about it?"

"I'll begin right away," said Bobby, "if you'll show me how."

And he did.

I wish you could have seen him digging. Such enthusiasm, such persistence! Early in the morning, before he went to school, Bobby was out at work, and back on the job again in the afternoon when he came home. Yard after yard he worked his way down the garden, with never a grumble or complaint and with never any need for anyone to keep him at it. He worked as though he loved it, as though he wanted to dig the garden better than anyone had ever dug it before. In fact, so smooth did he make the surface of the soil that it soon began to look like a big brown table.

Daddy was delighted and said he would rather have Bobby dig the garden than anybody else, at which Bobby swelled up with pride and satisfaction and went on digging harder and faster than ever. In fact, his mother sometimes had a big job to get him to come in to supper.

More than once he stayed out till after darkness had fallen, and everyone wondered how he could still see where to

◀ Painting by Harry Baerg

Yard after yard Bobby worked his way down the garden, with never a grumble or complaint.

put his fork.

At last the long, hard task was finished, and what joy was in Bobby's heart when he came in one day and said, "It's all done, Dad!"

Then came the still happier moment when Dad paid up.

Bobby put the money in his pocket, feeling rich. There were other jobs. Then the day came when Bobby and Dad went to the city and began to look for a bicycle. And was Bobby careful about his money? I should say so! He examined every machine with the utmost care and asked the poor salesmen in the shops all sorts of puzzling questions. Finally he made his decision, paid over his money, and walked out of the shop with his precious bicycle.

Because Daddy wouldn't let him ride it through the traffic, he had to push it most of the way home, but he didn't care, for it was sheer joy even to hold the saddle and the handle bars. And somehow, when he compared his bicycle with those of all the other boys in the neighborhood, he felt sure his was by far the best of all.

And if I may let you into a secret, Bobby still loves that bicycle, even though it is five years old, and he is much too big to ride it now. You see, digging for it made it worth so much more to him than if he had just received it as a present.

Maybe there's something you want ever so much and can't get because there's no money.

Why not try digging for it some way, too?

Brenda's Skates

IF THERE WAS one thing more than another that Brenda wanted for her birthday, it was a pair of roller skates. How she coaxed and coaxed for them! How she promised to be as good as gold for the next ten years if only Mother or Father would give her a pair!

In vain her mother explained that Brenda might not learn to use them as easily as other children, that she might fall many times and perhaps hurt herself before she could skate properly. Brenda wanted skates and that was that.

She thought about skates all day and dreamed about skates all night. She pictured herself skating to school and home again, skating to the stores for Mother, and skating all over the yard, of course. Was her birthday never going to come?

It came at last, and with it the precious parcel for which she had longed. Somehow, even before she opened it, she guessed there were skates inside. And there were. Beautiful new shiny skates. Just her size, too. What bliss! Brenda felt she had never been so happy in all her life.

And now to practice with them. Scarcely was breakfast over before she was out on the smooth concrete in front of the garage, strapping on the skates. At last, she thought, I am going to skate!

Eagerly she stood up. But only for a moment. Suddenly, to her great surprise, away went both her feet from under her. Down she went.

Bang!

"Mother!" she cried. "That hurt."

But Mother was indoors and did not notice. So Brenda stood up again. But hardly had she put one foot forward, when the other, for some reason, started running backward, and down she went again, this time on her face.

Bang!

This really hurt, and Brenda felt very much like crying. Slowly she got up once more and started to walk. But before she knew what was happening, bang! She was sitting on the concrete again.

Somehow she just couldn't do it. Up she got and down she went. It was a case of bump, bump, bump, and bang, bang, bang, until certain parts of her were quite sore. And she felt very sad. All her hopes of skating to school and to town like the other girls faded away.

As she sat on the concrete again, tears filled her eyes. She began to wish she had never asked for skates for her birthday. Why hadn't she asked for a new doll? or a new baby car-

riage? She wouldn't have got hurt then.

"Horrid old skates!" she cried, unstrapping them from her feet and throwing them inside the back door with a loud clatter.

"What's the matter?" called Mother. "Tired of skating already?"

"No," said Brenda crossly. "But I can't skate. I've fallen down so often I'm sore all over."

"Don't give up yet," said Mother. "You haven't started to learn. You must keep on trying till you succeed."

"Trying!" cried Brenda. "I've tried all I'm going to. I tell you, Mother, I'm sore. Sore! And I wish I had never asked for skates."

"Oh, tut, tut!" said Mother. "You are giving up altogether too easily."

"So would you," said Brenda, "if you had fallen on the same place as many times as I have this morning. Skating is not for me."

"But, Brenda," said Mother, "you are not going to let the other girls beat you, are you?"

"I don't care," said Brenda. "I can't skate. I just can't. So there!"

"You mustn't say 'can't,'" said Mother. "You can. But while skating comes easily to some, it is very hard for others.

Why, I don't know. Once I saw two children get skates for the first time. One put them on and sailed away just as if she had skated all her life. The other fell all over the place. But she tried and tried and tried again, until now she can skate as well as anybody else."

"Do you really think I could do it, too, if I tried?" asked Brenda.

"Of course," said Mother. "And I'll come along and help you."

"Now?"

"Yes, now," said Mother.

So on went the skates once more, and down went Brenda on the same sore spot. But she got up again and, leaning on Mother, went carefully forward.

Slowly, gradually, she got the idea of how to do it, how to balance herself, how to swing her weight gently, easily, this way and that.

Now and then, when all seemed to go wrong and she was sprawled all over the concrete, she wanted to give up and throw her skates away, but Mother would insist on her keeping going.

"You must never even think you can't do it," she said. "Just keep on trying, trying, trying, no matter how many times you fall. It's just like learning to do any difficult task in life. Never give up. Keep trying till you win."

So Brenda tried and tried again. Several days later she was skating round the concrete all by herself. Soon she was out on the sidewalk with the other girls, skating to school. By trying and trying and "sticking it out" she made her dream come true.

Dennis and the
Dive Bombers

IT LOOKED AS IF all the little boys in the neighborhood were going off to war. Dennis stood at the gate of his home and watched with wide-open eager eyes as they hurried by.

Some of them carried wooden guns over their shoulders; some had wooden swords; and others had pointed sticks that were supposed to be spears.

"Where are you going?" he called to some of the boys he knew.

"Come on!" they cried excitedly. "We're going to fight the enemy."

"Who's the enemy?" asked Dennis.

"We've found a wasps' nest out in the woods, and we're all going out to do battle with them."

"Mom!" Dennis cried as he ran indoors. "May I go to war with all the other boys?"

"Whatever's this nonsense?" asked Mother.

"They're all going out to the woods to fight the wasps, and they all have swords and guns and things. Let me go too— please, Mom."

◀ Painting by Vernon Nye, © Review and Herald

Two days later Dennis saw the boys going by the house again, just as they had done before, each one with his "weapon" of war.

Just then Daddy came on the scene and asked, just as Mother had, "What's all this nonsense?" And when he heard about it, he said that Dennis was not to go under any circumstances.

"It's a very foolish errand," he said. "Wasps can be very dangerous enemies, and one must be properly prepared to fight them. You can't hope to succeed with pieces of wood. No, Dennis, you can't go."

So that was that, and Dennis had to content himself with standing at the gate waiting for the boys to come back.

After what seemed an age, the boys came rushing past, waving their weapons in the air and shouting about their great victory, although just what they had done to the wasps he never did find out.

Two days later he saw the boys going by the house again, just as they had done before, each one with his "weapon" of war.

"Come on, Dennis," they cried. "Don't be a sissy!"

"Father says I mustn't come," he said.

"Oh, come on," they called; "he won't mind. It's going to be great fun."

Dennis wavered. He could go with the boys and get back without Daddy's knowing anything about it, for he was away at his office and wouldn't be back for hours. Mom was out too. It would be such fun to go with the others, and he did so want to find out how they fought wasps with wooden swords and spears.

So picking up a piece of wood to make a weapon for himself, he sallied forth to the battle.

On reaching the woods, some of the bigger boys began searching about for a wasps' nest, and it was not long before one of them called, "I have one. Here it is. And my, aren't they big fellows!"

They *were* big fellows. Actually, they were not wasps at all but hornets, and before long *they* were going into battle,

while the poor boys were running pell-mell in every direction.

One of the hornets lit on poor Dennis, stinging him on his upper lip just under his nose. In a few moments there was a huge painful swelling.

How he wished as he hurried homeward that he had not disobeyed his daddy! What would he say? And could anything Daddy might do to him be worse than the awful pain he was suffering?

When Mother saw what had happened, she was so frightened that she took him to the doctor for treatment. Dennis suffered so much that Daddy felt he had had more than sufficient punishment. But one day when Dennis was almost better Daddy said, "Well, Dennis, so the boys didn't win that battle they went out to fight."

"No," said Dennis. "The enemy had too many dive bombers. We couldn't do a thing."

"I can think of another reason," said Daddy. "Two of them, in fact."

"What?" asked Dennis.

"First, you didn't have proper equipment—no antiaircraft guns; and second, you acted without orders."

"Maybe you're right, Daddy," said Dennis.

And of course he was.

The Secret of Happiness

THE RADIO WEATHER REPORT said that snow was coming. This was good news for Joe and Gerald. It set them ablaze with energy.

They had often talked about making sleds for themselves, but so far had never done so. The good news about the snow made them decide to make one each, and so they eagerly began the task.

Every moment they could spare from their schoolwork the boys spent in the shed in Gerald's back yard sawing, planing, hammering, until at last to their great joy the sleds were completed and ready for the snow to fall.

But it did not come. Probably the clouds were blown away after the weather experts had looked at them. However that may be, the sad fact is that for many days there were two sleds in the shed with nothing to slide them on.

School closed for Christmas, and still there was no snow. Day after day went by cold and wet. There seemed about as much prospect of snow as of a heat wave. The boys gave up hope and wished they had never taken the trouble to make their sleds.

At last Christmas Eve arrived and with it came a sudden change. The rain stopped, the thermometer went down with a rush, and a strong wind arose.

"Something is going to happen," said Joe, as he went to bed that night. And he was right.

In the morning the clouds had gone, and the rising sun glistened on a vast expanse of snow. A heavy fall had covered the whole landscape with a glorious white mantle—just what they were hoping for.

Gerald was overjoyed. As soon as he awoke he guessed what had happened, for he could see the reflection of the snow on the ceiling. He leaped out of bed, dressed as quickly as he could, and rushed down the garden to the shed where the precious sleds had been stored so long. He hauled them both over the snow up to the house and then ran off to find Joe.

How happy they were! This was better than their highest expectations. No Christmas Day could have started more joyously for them. They decided that they would go off at once to a neighboring hill and have all the fun they had dreamed of.

They trotted off down the street dragging their sleds behind them. School friends shouted to them, all eager to share in the fun.

"Lucky fellows," they cried; "can we have a ride on your sled?"

"Not now," cried Joe and Gerald, "we're going off by ourselves today."

"Lend us one of your sleds," cried another.

"Nothing doing!" shouted Joe. "You should have made one for yourself."

Ralph Morton, the lame boy, waved his hand cheerfully from his window, and wished them lots of fun.

"Nice of him, wasn't it?" said Gerald.

"Yes," said Joe, " 'specially as he can never hope to pilot a sled of his own."

Just then they passed Madge Green's house. They had always been friendly with her and her little sisters. She greeted them cheerfully as usual and wished them a happy Christmas.

"Wish I could come for a slide," she said, "but I can't today. I'm helping Mother all I can, so that she can have a really happy Christmas."

The boys passed on. Soon they were out of the town and climbing the hill dragging their sleds behind them. Then they prepared their slide and the fun began.

Swish! Away they went down the hill. Then up to the top
again. Then another glorious slide. So they played together
for a couple of hours.

After a while, however, Joe noticed a change coming over
Gerald's face.

"What's up, Gerald?" asked Joe with some concern as they
climbed the hill together, this time a bit more slowly.

"Nothing much," said Gerald, "only somehow I'm not getting as much fun out of this as I thought I would."

"Aren't you?" said Joe. "I'm not, either. Of course, it's nice in a way, yet I don't feel comfortable. I wonder why it is."

"Funny we should both feel the same way," said Gerald, "isn't it?"

"Very funny," said Joe, as they trudged on up to the top.

Swish! Down they went again.

On the way up next time they talked about their strange feelings again.

"I think I know what's the matter," said Joe.

"What?" asked Gerald.

"I keep thinking about Ralph."

"So do I," said Gerald. "And Madge and the others. I wish we hadn't left them behind. Mean of us, wasn't it?"

"Yes," said Joe.

There was silence again as they climbed slowly upward.

"I think we'll have only one more," said Joe.

"All right," said Gerald.

They had the last slide, and then turned toward home. On the way they talked of how they would spend the afternoon. As they reached the town they began calling at the homes of some of their friends who had no sleds. What Gerald and Joe said to them seemed to make them very happy.

Dinner was scarcely over when there was a loud knock at their front door. Running out, Joe and Gerald found a happy, excited group of children waiting for them.

"Hurrah!" they all cried when they saw the two boys. "I'll be first," said one, and "Me, me, me, first!" called another.

Then sorting the visitors out, Joe and Gerald put two or three of them on each sled, and took them for rides up and down the street. Oh, the shrieks of joy! How they all did laugh and yell!

All the afternoon they kept it up—except for a game of snowball now and then—giving rides to all the children in turn, until at last, too weary to run anymore, Joe and Gerald sent them all home and put the hard-worked sleds back in the shed.

Sticking Pins
Into Billy

WILLIAM ARNOLD CROKER, known to the other boys in the town as "Billy," was a bright lad, but he had one fault. He thought so much of himself that his hat would hardly go on his head.

Billy's skill in games made him a natural leader of the boys, but they all secretly disliked him because he was always bragging about the wonderful things he could do. He never had time to listen to what the other boys had to say, but would always interrupt them with an account of some experience he had had. If someone said he had seen a big frog, Billy would say, "That's nothing; last week I saw a frog much bigger than that."

At last the other boys became tired of his boasting, and began to talk over ways and means of putting an end to it. As Tommy Walters said, Billy was swollen up with pride as big as a balloon, and it was high time somebody stuck a nice big pin into him.

But how to do it was another question. Some of the boys suggested ducking him in the river; but Billy was quite a strong boy, and none of the others wanted to take the risk of a personal quarrel with him. Then Tommy struck on a bright idea.

"I know of something better than that," he said. "It wouldn't be kind to put him in the river, and it wouldn't do him much good anyhow. Have you ever thought what is the matter with Billy?"

The others crowded around. "No, what?" they asked. They were in a mood to try anything.

"I'll tell you. You've all noticed how Billy seems to win all our games," said Tommy. "That's the trouble with him; he thinks we're no good, and that he can always beat us. I'm tired of his superior airs. If we are going to stop his bragging, we must learn to play better ourselves."

"Pretty good sense," said another boy. "If we could make Billy lose every game for a few weeks, he would soon change his tune."

"You're right," said Tommy, "but it's up to us to beat him. Why not practice some of our games on the quiet, and surprise Billy?"

"But we can't all win," said a pale-faced, timid youngster;

"and I don't see how we can practice all the games we play."

"Of course we can't all practice everything at once," said Tommy. "No; but let one or two practice running, some jumping, and others marbles. I'm going to practice so I can throw him out at first base the next time we play."

"Great!" laughed the others. "Let's do it."

Tommy's idea certainly did put new life into those boys. Their mothers and teachers soon began to wonder what was the matter with them, for nearly all of them began to practice hard at the games they had chosen in their secret meeting.

Billy, too, noticed it but did not suspect that all this effort was directed against him. As the days went by, he began to notice the results of the plan. In running races he had always been able to keep an easy lead, but a few of the boys now began to keep up with him, and some passed him. Instead of always winning, he learned what it means to lose.

When the school field day came around, so many pins were stuck into Billy that he was reduced to almost normal size. Billy had not bothered to practice for any of the events because he felt so certain of success. The other boys, however,

had worked very hard with but one purpose in view, and they won. Poor Billy did not win a single race.

He felt very bad about it, but was sure he would be able to regain his lost reputation at the baseball game that was to follow the field events, for he prided himself on being a very good hitter.

This ball game was always a big affair, at least in the boys' eyes, for it was held on the town diamond, and usually there were many spectators.

Billy was up first. He told the boys that he was going to make at least ten runs, and that they had better keep their eye on the town clock, for he was going to hit a ball right in the middle of it. Then, carrying his bat with a real swagger, he strolled across the field as if he were a professional. But much to his surprise, Billy fanned out.

In the next inning Tommy was up first. He saw at once that his great opportunity had come. After all he had said to the other boys, he knew what he must do.

Tommy had been practicing batting and fielding every morning and evening. In the morning, before his fa-

ther went to work, Tommy would get him out into the vacant lot next to the house to pitch him a few balls. After school he would get one of the boys to play with him. Then in the evening after supper his father would throw him a few more, until his eye and timing were nearly perfect, and he could hit curves as hard as straight balls. So now he really felt ready for the big game.

Tommy walked out to the batter's box with more assurance than ever before. The pitcher shot him a fast ball. But Tommy was ready; he had been training his eye carefully, and he was sure of his swing. To the surprise of all, he hit the ball away out, and before the left fielder recovered the ball, Tommy was rounding third. The left fielder threw to Billy, who was catching, but Billy dropped the ball, and Tommy slid in home—a home run.

Tommy made two more home runs that day, one in the last inning with two out and two men on base, partly because Billy, who was really a good player, lost his nerve at being

surpassed, and partly because he worked so hard to succeed. Billy failed to make a single run in the game.

At the close of the game they all crowded around Tommy and proclaimed him hero of the day.

As for Billy, no one would have thought he was the same boy who had walked so confidently onto the diamond a couple of hours before.

"How about the town clock?" piped a small voice.

"And how about those ten runs?" ventured a bolder voice among the boys.

But Billy only walked away with his head down. That was the last "pin" that Billy needed to have stuck into him. No one ever heard him boasting again.

The Worth of a Smile

HOW MUCH IS A SMILE WORTH? A penny? A quarter? A hundred dollars?

Well, it's worth something, isn't it?

It surely is, but somehow you could never fix a price for a smile, could you? To do so would spoil its value at once.

Yet sometimes a smile is very valuable.

Many years ago there lived on one of the very poor streets of New York a little girl called Hannah. She was eleven years old and her cheerful little face often brought gladness to sad people who saw her on the street.

One day Hannah went to a children's program at a nearby church. She had been there many times before to attend meetings of various kinds; but this time she was to take part in a program herself. You can imagine how pleased she was about it.

Now, it so happened that in the audience that afternoon was a well-known doctor, one of the supporters of that church. Whether or not he was feeling lonely or sad that day will never be known, but somehow as he looked at Hannah's dear little face, his heart was touched. Then she turned and looked straight at him and smiled! He thought he had never seen anything so lovely before. He left the hall a happier and better man.

And he never forgot that smile. It lived with him every day until he died.

When his will was read, his executors were astonished to learn that he had left all his money—and he was a very rich man—not to any relatives, for he had none; not to any hospital or mission, as he might have done, but, using his own words, "to those who have given me happiness during my lifetime."

On the list was Hannah's name, the little girl who had smiled at him in the church program twenty years before. He left her $150,000!

Think of that—$150,000 for a smile!

I can almost hear you saying, "I wish my smiles were worth as much as that." They are! But not in money.

Think of the happiness they bring to Mother and Father. Your smiles help them bear their burdens more easily, and make them live longer, too. Isn't that worth something?

Smiles make the wheels of a home move so much more smoothly, while frowns and scowls and pouts are like sand and gravel thrown into the works.

Who does not love the boy or girl who smiles when things go wrong—when other children annoy them or they are hurt while playing games? Such smiles are worth much more than money.

Suppose you smile someday at someone who is very sad and discouraged, and make him smile, too; what is that worth? You may never know, but it may mean everything to him—the turning of a corner on life's dark and lonely road. And there are lots of people today like this, people who have given up hope that anybody will smile at them again. As the familiar hymn says—

"There are hearts that are drooping in sorrow
  today,
 There are souls under shadow the while;
Oh, the comfort from God you can gently
  convey,
 And brighten the way with a smile!"

Won't you try to see how much good you can do with your smiles? You will be repaid in happiness untold.

How Grandma Came
for Christmas

AT LAST THE DAY HAD COME to open the money boxes! How long it had taken to fill them! What hard work it had meant, what careful saving, what giving up of candy and nice ribbons and special treats! To Hilda and Mona it had seemed as though they would *never* be allowed to open them, and sometimes they had even said it wasn't worth-while putting the money in.

But at last the day had come! It was a week before Christmas, and of course everybody was wanting all the money he could find for presents and new dresses and things. How glad the children were that they had heeded their mother and had kept the boxes unopened till now! Mother was right, after all.

Click! went the key in Mona's little cash box, and there inside she saw the pile of pennies, nickels, dimes, quarters, and one half dollar. What joy! She counted it all up, and Hilda counted it afterward, just to make sure it was right. Four dollars and fifty-one cents! What a lot of money for a little girl!

"Now you open yours," said Mona. "I wonder who has the most?"

Hilda's was a strange-looking money box, and it certainly held money tightly. It was such a job to get it out. She had to use a knife, but as she poked it in, out came the pennies, nickels, dimes, quarters, and two half dollars. It was a lovely sight.

"Oh!" said Mona, "you have more than I!"

"It looks like it," said Hilda. "Let's count it up. One, two, three. Why, I believe there's more than five dollars!"

And so there was. It came to $5.28. How happy they were! Never had they had so much money to spend all at once.

Then came the big question. What should they spend it on? Soon they realized how little they had really saved.

There were so many things they wanted to buy, and most of them cost more than they had saved.

Mona thought she would like to get a pretty dress, but how far would $4.51 go? Hilda's first thought was for a beau-

tiful handbag, the kind with two pockets in the middle and a mirror. But again, how far would $5.28 go? Then they talked of other things they would like—so many things—but try as they would they could not stretch their money nearly far enough to cover all their desires.

"I'm getting tired of trying to decide," said Hilda. "This money is a bother."

"Do you know," said Mona, "I wonder whether the trouble is that we are trying to spend it all on ourselves?"

Hilda sat very quiet and still. "Perhaps it is," she said.

"Just for fun," said Mona, "let's try to think how we could spend it on some other people."

"Mom, for instance," said Hilda.

"Yes, or even Grandma," said Mona.

" All right. You write down what you would buy for them and I'll do the same."

So they both found pencil and paper and began to write. Hilda soon made a long list—long enough to use up her $5.28 many times over.

"You don't seem to have put down much, Mona," she said, looking at her paper.

"No," said Mona, "but I've got an idea! I've thought of something that would be a beautiful present for both Mom and Grandma."

"Come on, then, let's have it," said Hilda.

"Well," said Mona, "you know how Mom has been longing to have Grandma come down here to stay with her for a while? Well, the only reason Grandma doesn't come is that she can't afford the fare and Mom can't afford to sent it to her. Wouldn't it be wonderful if we were to send Grandma her fare ourselves, and invite her down to surprise Mom?"

"Mona, you are a genius!" said Hilda. "I should enjoy that much more than a new handbag. Let's do it right now."

"Isn't it just lovely?" said Mona. "I'm so glad you like the idea. I'd much rather see Mom happy than have a new dress.

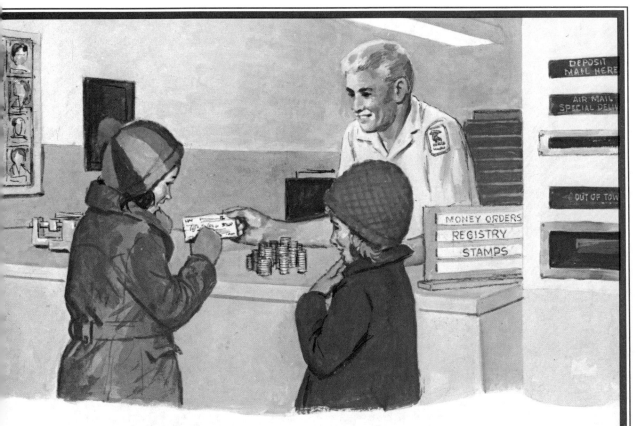

Let's get a pen and some writing paper. You'll write the letter, won't you?"

"All right," said Hilda. "You tell me what to say."

So together they wrote to Grandma:

"Our dear Grandma,

"We all want you very much to come down here for Christmas. Mona and I have been saving up for a long time to pay your fare, and you will find it in this letter. Don't lose it, and be sure to come soon. We shall expect you next week.

"With lots of love from Hilda and Mona."

"Oh, Mona," said Hilda when she had finished writing; "whatever will Mom say when Grandma comes?"

"Oh, that's part of the fun. She'll be so pleased and surprised she won't know what to do with herself."

Picking up their money and putting on their coats, the two went down to the post office, bought a postal money order for $9, and mailed it to Grandma. Chuckling all over

and enjoying their secret immensely, they returned home to await the big surprise.

For the next few days the girls could not settle down to anything. Every footstep made them jump, and every creak of the front gate gave them a start. They felt inside themselves that they had done something big and beautiful, not unmixed with mischief, and they just couldn't keep still.

Every now and then they would burst out laughing, for no apparent reason whatever.

Mother wondered what could have gone wrong with them. They often had innocent little secrets they tried to keep from her, but this was rather mysterious.

Then at last came a different knock at the door.

"Hilda, there's someone at the door," called Mother. "Go and see who it is."

But Hilda guessed that the great moment had come, and she wanted Mother to have the surprise they had planned so long. Making up a hurried excuse, she said, "Do please go yourself, Mom."

So Mother hurried to the door, rather hot and bothered—thinking it was the postman or the milkman. She opened the door sharply—and there stood Grandma, with her handbags and trunk, as though she had come to stay a month.

"Well, well!" cried Mother. "Whoever—whatever! Isn't this wonderful! But how did you come? Who could have dreamed you would be here for Christmas!"

"Why, didn't you expect me?" said Grandma, equally surprised.

There was a loud chuckle in the background.

"Ah, those two young scamps," said Grandma. "I guess they are at the bottom of this."

Then came the explanations, and everybody was happy.

After the excitement had died down, Grandma called the children to her and, slowly and mysteriously, opened her trunk.

◄ Painting by Manning de V. Lee

Mamma hurried to the door, rather hot and bothered. She opened the door sharply—and there stood Grandma with her handbags and trunk.

"I'm not too old to use my fingers yet," she said, pulling out a couple of packages. "Here's a little dress I've been making for Mona, and I've got a wee handbag made all of beads for Hilda."

"Oh, no!" cried the girls together, looking at each other in amazement.

"Why, don't you want them?" asked Grandma.

"Want them! I should say we do! They are just perfect," said Hilda. "But how did you know? They are the very things we were going to buy for ourselves with the money we had saved in our boxes."

"Well, did you ever!" exclaimed Grandma. "Do you know, girls," she said, "I believe the good old Book is right when it says, 'He that hath pity upon the poor lendeth unto the Lord; and that which he hath given will he pay him again.'"

Tommy's Trucks

TOMMY WAS ONLY a very little boy, but he had a will of his own. That is, he liked to have his own way, and he didn't like to do what he was told.

Now, Tommy had some beautiful little trucks and cars, toy ones, of course, that Daddy had bought for him from time to time. He must have had a dozen trucks at least, and as for the cars, well, there were blue cars and orange cars and green cars and yellow cars. Some were racers and some were nice little compacts. There was an ambulance too, and a fire truck, which was Tommy's special delight.

Tommy loved to play with all his precious trucks and cars on the front porch, though sometimes he would take them out to the driveway that led to the garage. He would make "roads" for them in the gravel and imagine that they were real.

Of course, Tommy was supposed to bring them indoors every evening after he had finished playing, but that was something he never wanted to do. He would say that it didn't matter; that he would bring them in later; that it would be all right to leave them out all night ready for him to play with in the morning.

One afternoon he made up his mind that he wouldn't bring them in. "No," he said, "I'll bring them in after a while. I'm not ready yet."

"But, Tommy," urged Mother, "something may happen to them out there. They might be stolen; a car might run over them."

"They'll be all right," said Tommy. "Nothing has happened to them so far."

"But you'd be very sorry if something did," said Mother. "You know you would."

"I'll bring them in after supper."

"It'll be dark then. Bring them in now."

"Later on."

"I said now, Tommy."

"All right."

But Tommy didn't bring them in. He went to the front door and then forgot all about them.

By and by, after dark, two big headlights came flashing up the drive. It was Daddy coming home.

"Oh, look out for my trucks and cars!" shouted Tommy.

Alas, it was too late.

Crunch! Crunch! Crunch!

Daddy's big car had run over them all.

The ambulance was flat as a pancake; the fire truck was completely wrecked; the racing cars would never race again.

"Oh, look what you've done! Look what you've done!" cried Tommy rushing outside, shining a flashlight over all his ruined toys and sorrowfully picking them up, one by one.

"I'm sorry," said Daddy. "I'm dreadfully sorry."

"You don't need to be," said Mother. "Tommy was told to bring them in long ago."

"Oh, my poor cars!" wailed Tommy. "Oh, my poor fire truck! Why did you run over them?"

"You should know why," said Mother. "Remember how many times I spoke to you about them?"

◄ Painting by Jack White

Tommy loved to play with his precious trucks and cars on the driveway.

"I forgot," cried Tommy, "and now they're all smashed up. There isn't one whole one left. Oh, what'll I do?"

It was a sad procession that went indoors.

"I suppose," whispered Daddy to Mother, "I'll have to go downtown again right now."

"Not yet," whispered Mother. "Let us wait and see whether he has learned his lesson."

They did not have to wait long.

Tommy had learned his lesson all right. Indeed he decided to pick up his toys when Mother said to, *just when she said it.*

Perhaps I should add that, all in good time, Daddy and Tommy *did* go on a little trip downtown together, Tommy looking very happy and excited on the front seat of Daddy's car.

Can you guess what they brought back with them?

Saved From the Flood

NIGHT HAD FALLEN. Everybody in the little town was asleep. Everybody, that is, except the policeman, who was keeping his watch all alone in the police station.

Nobody dreamed that danger was near. No serious trouble had come to the town in years and years. There was no sign of trouble now, except that the level of the water in the river was a little higher than usual. But then, the water often rose and fell without anyone's noticing it. Sometimes, especially in the hot, dry summer, the river was merely a little trickle, way down at the bottom of its forty-foot-high banks.

The night wore on. There was no sound save the beating of the rain on the roofs and roadways, and the occasional barking of a dog.

Suddenly the telephone rang sharp and loud in the police station.

Startled a bit, the policeman picked up the receiver. "Hello," he said.

The words that came over the phone shocked him.

"Flood warning!" said a voice. "Lots of water rushing your

way. Will reach you in thirty minutes. Get the people out of all houses on low-lying ground. There's no time to lose. Hurry!"

A flood! In thirty minutes! How little time to warn everybody! How quickly he must work!

The policeman sounded the alarm, and in an instant the whole town was alive. A few minutes later men were hurrying to the houses down by the river, waking the sleeping families and helping them move what they could of their goods to higher ground. There just wasn't time to salvage many things.

Some of the people, just roused from sleep, didn't want to move, especially in the middle of the night, with rain pouring down. They couldn't believe that a flood was only a few minutes away. But the policemen and the firemen and other friends hurried them out to safety.

Then it came. About one o'clock in the morning a wall of water, full of uprooted trees, broken houses, and dead animals, rushed by. On its churning surface were tables, chairs, pianos, oil drums, and even cars! It hit the bridge in the middle of town and carried it away as though it had been made of paper. It overflowed its banks and filled all the low-lying land nearby. Some of the houses which people had left but a few minutes before were lifted off their foundations and sent sailing downstream. Others simply collapsed, fell apart, and were carried away.

By this time hundreds of people were standing on high ground near the river, peering through the darkness at the terrible scene before them. How glad they were that nobody was in those houses that were being smashed and carried away by the flood!

Nobody?

"Look!" cried someone, pointing over the swirling water. "Surely that was a light! Over there; look!"

"It can't be," said others. "There's nobody there; and there's no light anyway."

"But there it is again! Look! It must be a candle. Somebody keeps lighting it, and it blows out."

"So it is! You're right. Whose house is it?"

"That's Mrs. Smith's house. Her husband's in the Army, and she had four little children with her. Didn't anybody warn them?"

No, nobody did. Somehow, in the darkness and the excitement, that house had been missed. Now it was surrounded by wild, rushing water which threatened any moment to carry it away.

"Give me a rope!" cried some brave soul. "I'll swim over there!"

They tied a rope round the man, and he set off. But he couldn't get anywhere near. It was impossible. The swift current carried him away, and it was only with great difficulty that he was hauled back. Another man offered to go but he also failed. A third made the attempt, but exhausted, had to give up.

Meanwhile, out there in the darkness a brave mother was making a gallant fight for life and for the lives of her children.

As no one had called to warn her of the coming flood, she and her children were all fast asleep when the first rush of water came sweeping into their house. Awakened by shouts and the roar of the flood waters going by, she jumped out of bed, to find herself standing in two feet of water, which covered the bedroom floor and was fast rising. Suddenly realizing what had happened, she grabbed her four children and lifted them one by one onto the top of a large cupboard. Then as the water rose above the beds, the table, the chairs, she clambered up on top of the cupboard herself, taking with her a candle and matches, a dry blanket, a bottle of milk, a knife, an old chisel, and, of all things, a flatiron!

Now they were all huddled together on top of the cupboard, wondering just how high the water would rise. Then it was that this dear, brave mother began to pray that God would spare her and her children, and if not, let them die together.

An hour passed by. Two hours. It was now three o'clock in the morning. They could feel the water close to the top of the cupboard. Suddenly one of the inside walls of the house gave way and fell with a great splash.

"The end must be near now," this brave mother said to herself. But she was not ready to give up yet.

Now it was that she made use of the tools she had so wisely brought with her, thinking that she might in some way need them.

Just over their heads was the ceiling, made of thin boards. "If I could just cut through it," she said to herself, "we could climb up on the rafters. Then we would be another two feet above the water."

Seizing the flatiron and the blunt chisel, she began chipping away at the board, splitting it off in little pieces until she had made a hole two feet long by nine inches wide. Through this tiny hole she pushed her children, one by one, telling each to sit astride a rafter. She was afraid they might

Mrs. Smith quickly lifted her four children, one by one, to the top of a large cupboard.

fall through the frail board if they were to stand on it. Then she pulled herself up through the hole and sat with them there, waiting, wondering, praying, while below, the water swirled through the house.

Four o'clock. Five o'clock. Six o'clock. It was getting light now. And what a scene! The great brown torrent was still surging by, with bits of broken houses and furniture floating on its surface.

Hundreds of people who had watched all night were looking anxiously at the one little house still standing in the midst of the flood. Only its roof could be seen now, with the tops of some of its windows. Surely everybody in it must have drowned long ago!

But no! As they look they see that somebody is cutting a hole in the roof!

The brave little mother is making her last attempt to save her children. She apparently is going to lift them out onto the roof if need be!

A shout goes up from the people and tears come to many eyes. But the little family is still in grave danger. At any moment the house could begin to come apart under the pressure of the swirling water.

"Let me try again," says a strong swimmer. "I think I can make it now."

They tie a rope around his waist and he sets off through the raging waters. He is swept downstream, but fights his way up again. At last, after a mighty effort, he reaches the house. Another shout goes up from the people anxiously watching on the bank. He has got there in time! The family may yet be saved.

Tying the rope securely, he makes his way in through a window. The large cupboard, on which the family had waited so long, and by which they had climbed into the loft, is gone. He signals back for a ladder. Soon another swimmer, aided by the rope, is on his way with one. Another swimmer follows. Soon one of them is seen coming from the house with a little girl on his shoulders.

Another mighty cheer rends the morning air. Then another and another as one by one the children are brought by strong hands along the rope, strained to the uttermost by the fury of the torrent.

Then, as all brave captains are the last to leave a sinking ship, so this dear mother is the last to leave her falling house. When all her four children have been taken to safety she comes out herself and, with the help of her rescuers, makes her way to land. What a cheer the people give for her! And she deserves it. Brave little mother!

I hope her children never forget how they were saved from death that dreadful night. It was a mother's faith against a flood.

Jimmy and the Jam Jars

JIMMY HAD A GREAT liking for jam. Indeed, he loved it. In this, of course, he was not very different from most other little boys of his age—and girls, too, for that matter. But Jimmy, well, he couldn't even look at a jam jar without feeling all stirred up inside.

Now, it so happened that one fine day Mother had spent the whole morning making strawberry jam. She had filled twenty or thirty jars, some large, some small, and by early afternoon they were all standing in neat rows in the top of her kitchen cabinet.

What a pleasing picture they made, with big strawberries clearly to be seen amid the thick red jelly.

Happy to think that her task was done, with all the dirty dishes and saucepans cleaned and put away, Mother decided to go out visiting for a little while.

"Jimmy," she said, as she came downstairs with her hat and coat on, "I'm going across to see Mrs. Brown for a few minutes. I'll be back soon. Be a good boy while I'm away."

"All right, Mother," said Jimmy. "Don't worry. I'll be real good, you'll see."

"You have plenty of things to play with, haven't you?"

"Oh, yes, Mother," said Jimmy. "I think I'll play with my trains."

"That's a good idea," said Mother. "And, by the way, I think it would be better for you not to go into the kitchen."

"All right, Mother. Why?"

"Oh, well," said Mother, thinking of her newly made jam, "just because—er—well, I think you had better not. Now, good-by, Jimmy, and be good."

"Good-by, Mother," said Jimmy, waving his hand and then running to play with his trains.

Unfortunately, Mother was gone much longer than she expected. It often happens that way, you know.

Meanwhile Jimmy got tired of playing with his trains and turned to his bricks, then to his trucks. At last he decided he didn't want to play with anything anymore, and started to walk around the house, looking for something to do.

From the kitchen there still came the sweet odor of newly

made jam, and Jimmy thought it was a very nice smell indeed. He went to the kitchen door and peeked in. Everything was very clean and tidy, and he could not see any particular reason why his mother should not want him to go in there. So in he went and wandered around.

As he walked about he kept saying to himself, "I wonder where Mom put all that jam."

Suddenly he looked upward, and, lo, there it was, all of it, on the three top shelves of the old-fashioned kitchen cabinet. The bright-red jars looked like rows of old-time soldiers such as one sees sometimes in picture books.

"What a fine lot of jam!" exclaimed Jimmy.

He looked and looked and looked.

"I wonder," he said to himself after a while, "if Mother would mind if I were to open the cupboard door and look at it a little closer?"

As Mother wasn't there to answer his question, he decided to answer it himself, and proceeded to carry a stool over to the base of the cabinet.

Now, Mother had an old-fashioned kitchen cabinet, made in two parts. There was a top half and a bottom half, and the one sat lightly on the other.

Unfortunately, Jimmy didn't know that.

Standing on the stool, he was just able to reach the knob on the glass door, which he gently pulled. The two doors swung open, revealing to Jimmy a wonderful array of jam jars.

"I wonder," he said to himself, "if Mother would mind if I were to taste just a little bit—just a very little bit. There is so much that I don't think Mother would even notice it, and I'm sure she wouldn't mind."

So Jimmy reached up and began trying to open one of the jam jars.

Alas! Just at that moment the stool slipped away from under his feet. To save himself, Jimmy clutched desperately

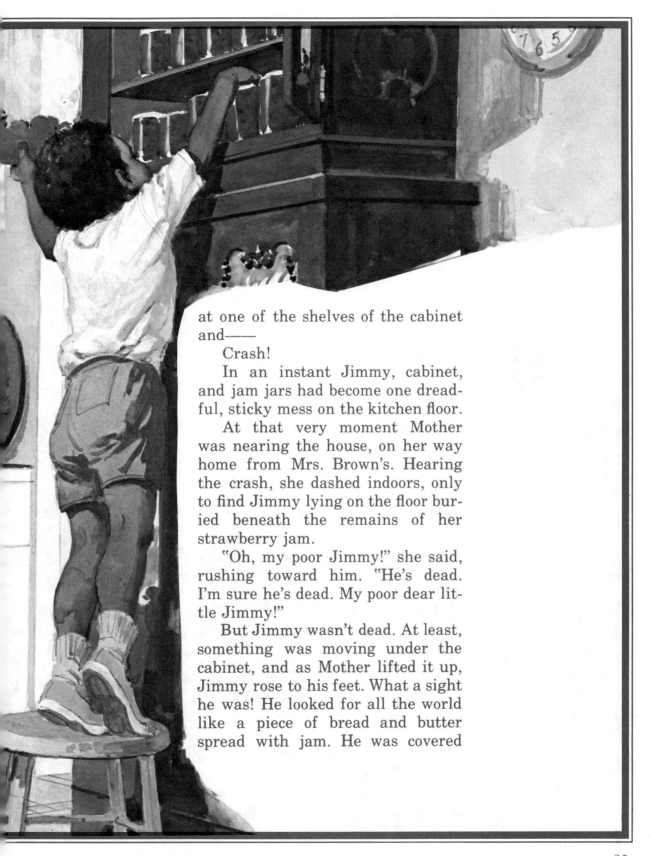

at one of the shelves of the cabinet
and——

Crash!

In an instant Jimmy, cabinet,
and jam jars had become one dreadful, sticky mess on the kitchen floor.

At that very moment Mother
was nearing the house, on her way
home from Mrs. Brown's. Hearing
the crash, she dashed indoors, only
to find Jimmy lying on the floor buried beneath the remains of her
strawberry jam.

"Oh, my poor Jimmy!" she said,
rushing toward him. "He's dead.
I'm sure he's dead. My poor dear little Jimmy!"

But Jimmy wasn't dead. At least,
something was moving under the
cabinet, and as Mother lifted it up,
Jimmy rose to his feet. What a sight
he was! He looked for all the world
like a piece of bread and butter
spread with jam. He was covered

with jam from head to foot. There was jam in his hair and jam on his shirt, jam on his trousers and jam on his shoes.

Mother took Jimmy over to the sink and began to wash the jam out of his eyes and ears. Then she found that he wasn't really hurt at all—not a single cut anywhere, despite all that broken glass!

Then a new note came into Mother's voice. She was cross and no doubt about it.

"You naughty little boy!" she cried. "How dare you disobey me like that! Look at all my jam! Look at my cabinet all broken to pieces! You bad boy, you!"

At this point Mother began walking towards the stairs, with Jimmy's hand held tightly in hers.

Just what happened upstairs I will leave you to imagine, but Jimmy told me—yes, he told me himself—that in all the years that have gone by since then he has never forgotten what happened that afternoon, and—what matters most of all—he has never, never disobeyed his mother from that day to this.

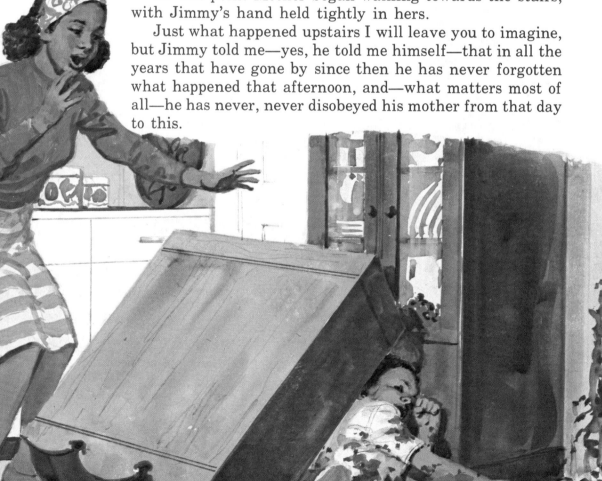

FOR SCHOOL-AGE CHILDREN
The Bible Story
This is the most accurate and complete set of children's Bible story books available. More than 400 Bible stories are included, with full color paintings at every page-opening. Unlike television, these stories introduce children to heroes you would be proud to have them imitate. These stories are also an excellent tool for loving parents who want their children to grow up making right decisions and making them with confidence. Ten volumes, hardcover.

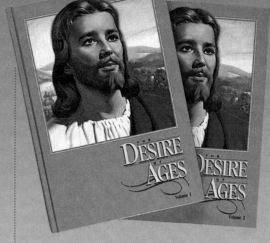

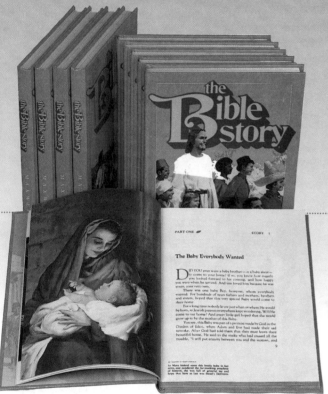

The Desire of Ages
This is E. G. White's monumental best-seller on the life of Christ. It is perhaps the most spiritually perceptive of the Saviour's biographies since the Gospel According to John. Here Jesus becomes more than a historic figure—He is the great divine-human personality set forth in a hostile world to make peace between God and man. Two volumes, hardcover.

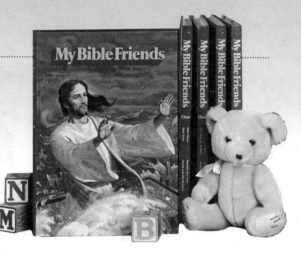

Uncle Arthur's Bedtime Stories
For years this collection of stories has been the center of cozy reading experiences between parents and children. Arthur Maxwell tells the real-life adventures of young children—adventures that teach the importance of character traits like kindness and honesty. Discover how a hollow pie taught Robert not to be greedy and how an apple pie shared by Annie saved her life. Five volumes, hardcover.

FOR PRESCHOOL CHILDREN
My Bible Friends
Imagine your child's delight as you read the charming story of Small Donkey, who carried tired Mary up the hill toward Bethlehem. Or of Zacchaeus the Cheater, who climbed a sycamore tree so he could see Jesus passing by. Each book has four attention-holding stories written in simple, crystal-clear language. And the colorful illustrations surpass in quality what you may have seen in any other children's Bible story book. Five volumes, hardcover. Also available in videos and audio cassettes.

MORE FAMILY READING

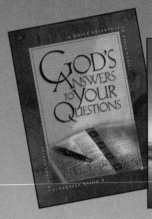

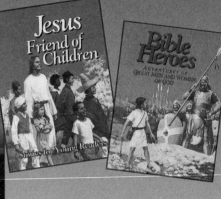

God's Answers to Your Questions
You ask the questions; it points you to Bible texts with the answers

He Taught Love
The true meaning hidden within the parables of Jesus

Jesus, Friend of Children
Favorite chapters from *The Bible Story*

Bible Heroes
A selection of the most exciting adventures from *The Bible Story*

The Storybook
Excerpts from Uncle Arthur's *Bedtime Stories*

My Friend Jesus
Stories for preschoolers from the life of Christ, with activity page

Food That Heal
Nutrition expert explains how to change your life by improving your diet

Plants That Heal
Unlocks the secrets of plants that heal the body and invigorate the mind

Choices: Quick and Healthy Cooking
Healthy meal plans you can make in a hurry

More Choices for a Healthy, Low-Fat You
All-natural meals you can make in 30 minutes

Tasty Vegan Delights
Exceptional recipes without animal fats or dairy products

Fun With Kids in the Kitchen Cookbook
Let your kids help with these healthy recipes

Health Power
Choices you can make that will revolutionize your health

Secret Keys
Character-building stories for children

Joy in the Morning
Replace disappointment and despair with inner peace and lasting joy

FOR MORE INFORMATION:
- write
  Home Health Education Service
  P.O. Box 1119
  Hagerstown, MD 21741
- or visit www.thebiblestory.com